ANNIE LEARNS TO RIDE

by JENNIFER BELL

J. A. ALLEN & CO. LTD.,
1, LOWER GROSVENOR PLACE, LONDON SW1W OEL

BRITISH LIBRARY CATALOGUING IN PUBLICATION DATA
BELL, JENNIFER
   ANNIE LEARNS TO RIDE
   1. ENGLISH CARTOONS
   I. TITLE
   741 5'942

   ISBN 0-85131-492-9

PUBLISHED IN GREAT BRITAIN BY
J.A. ALLEN & COMPANY LIMITED.
1. LOWER GROSVENOR PLACE,
BUCKINGHAM PALACE ROAD,
LONDON SW1W DEL

© JENNIFER BELL 1990

COLOUR REPRODUCTION BY
TENON & POLERT LTD.,
HONG KONG.

PRINTED AND BOUND BY
DAH HUA PRINTING PRESS CO. LTD.,
HONG KONG.

...AND IN DREAMS .... WHERE NOTHING IS IMPOSSIBLE .....

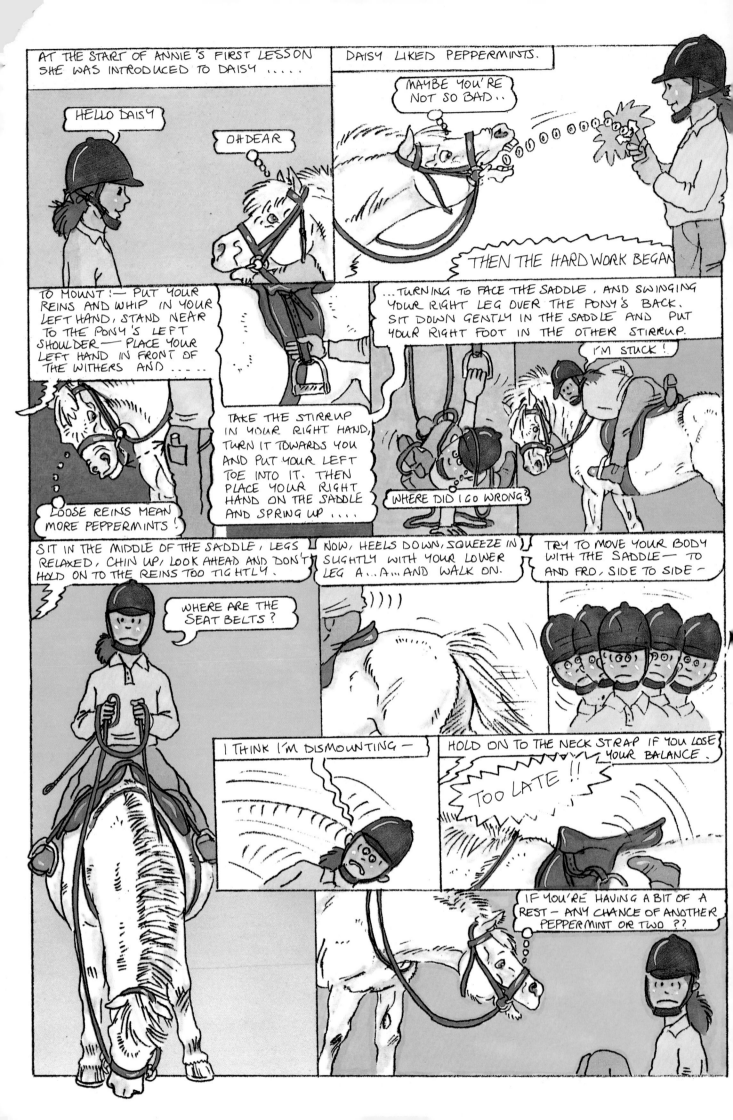

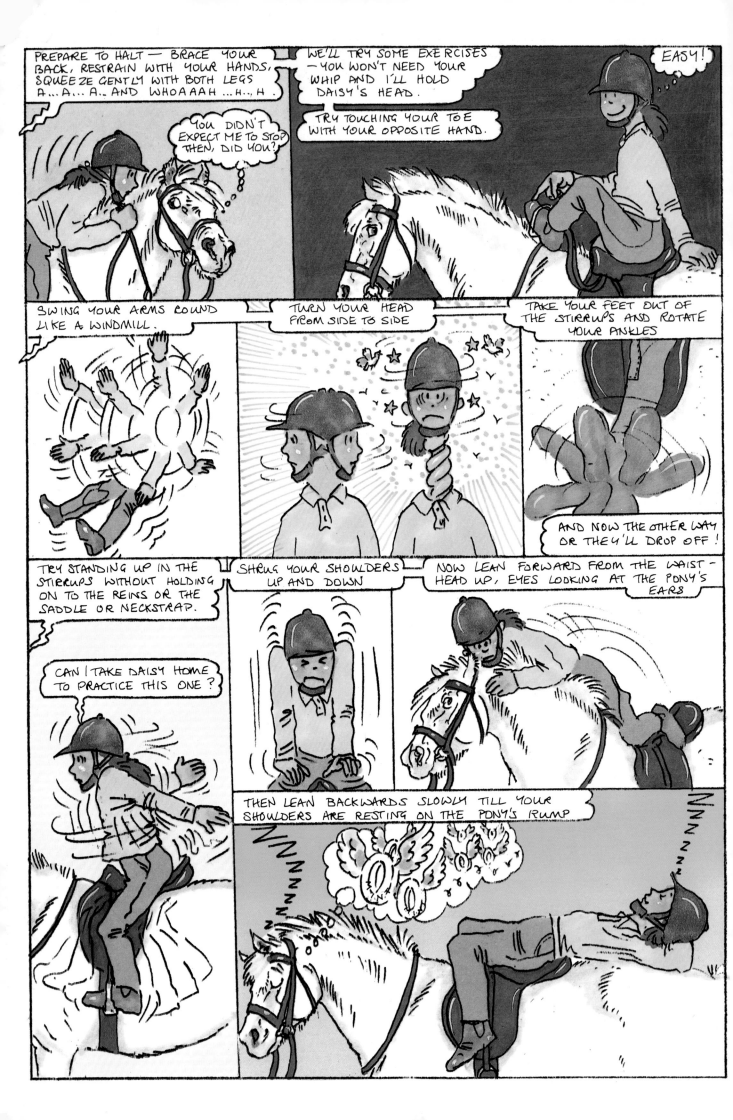

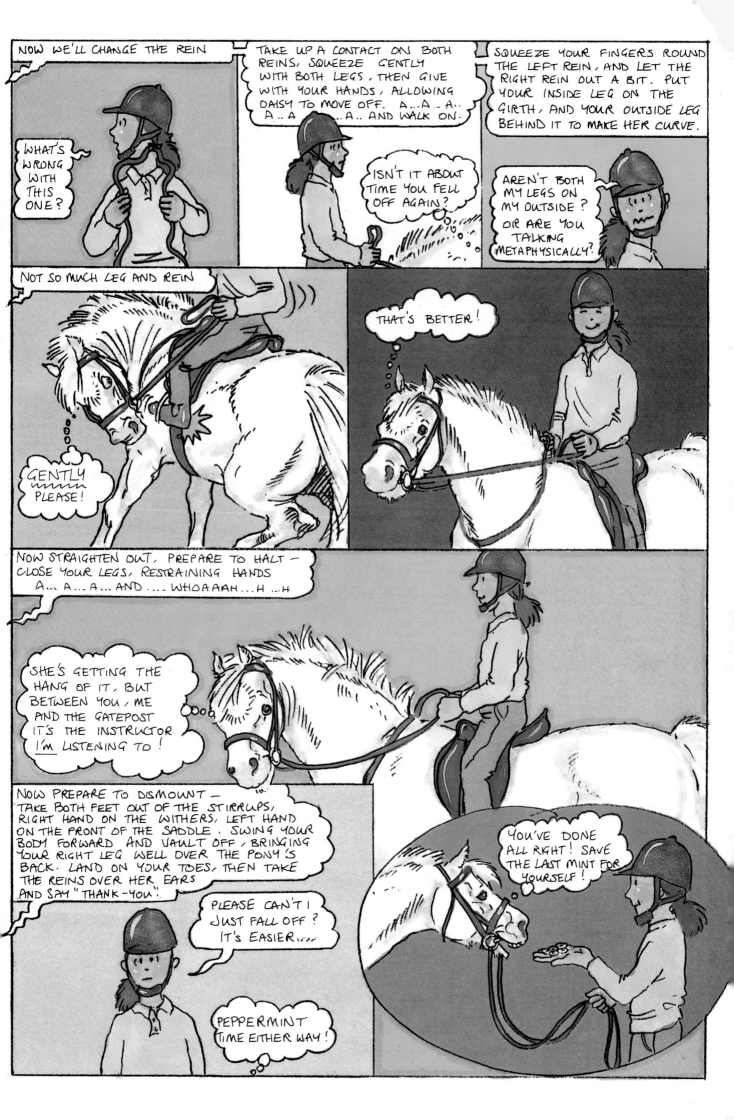

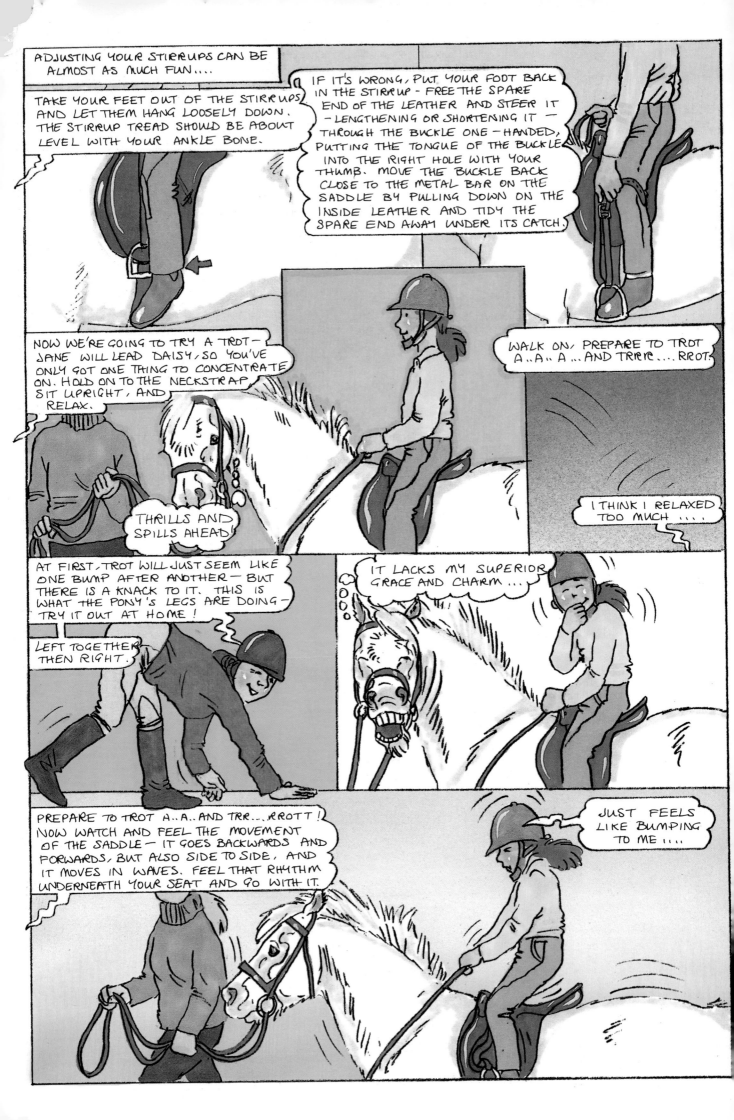

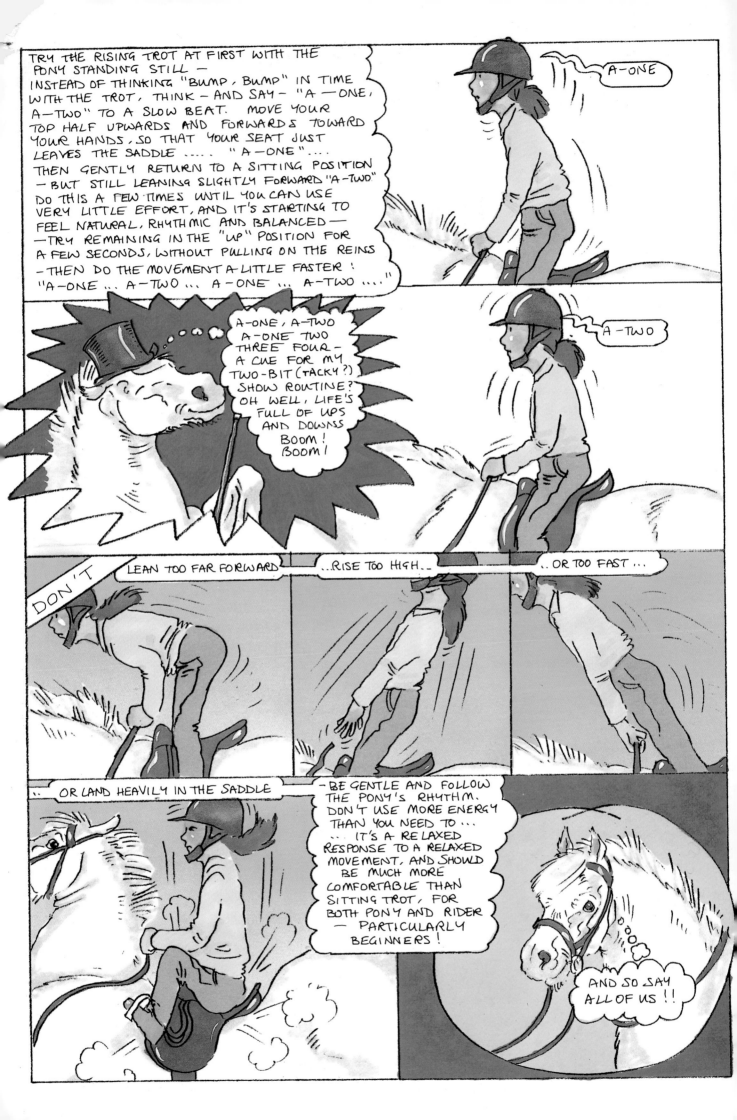

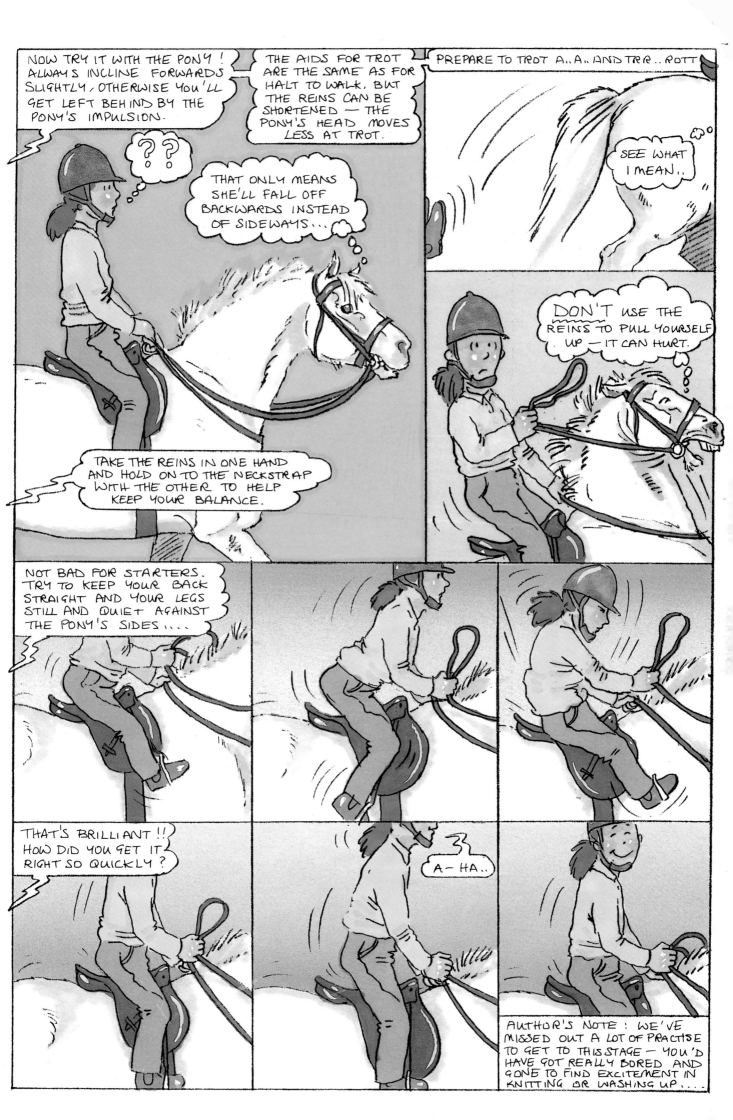

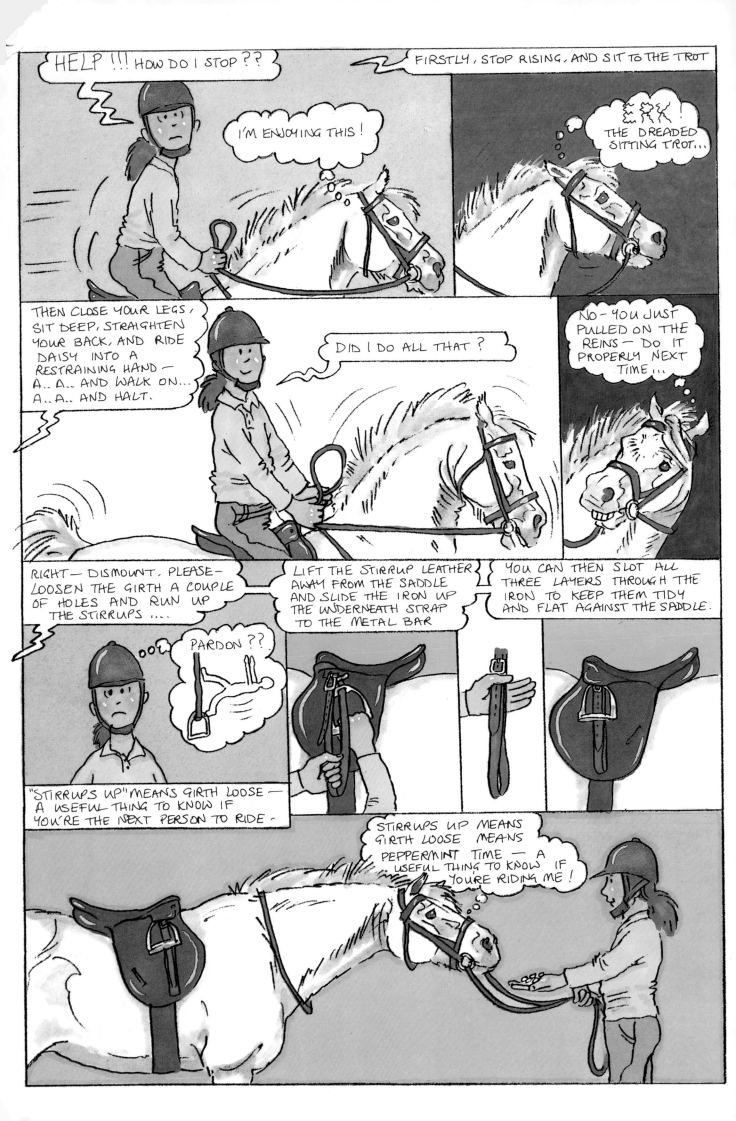

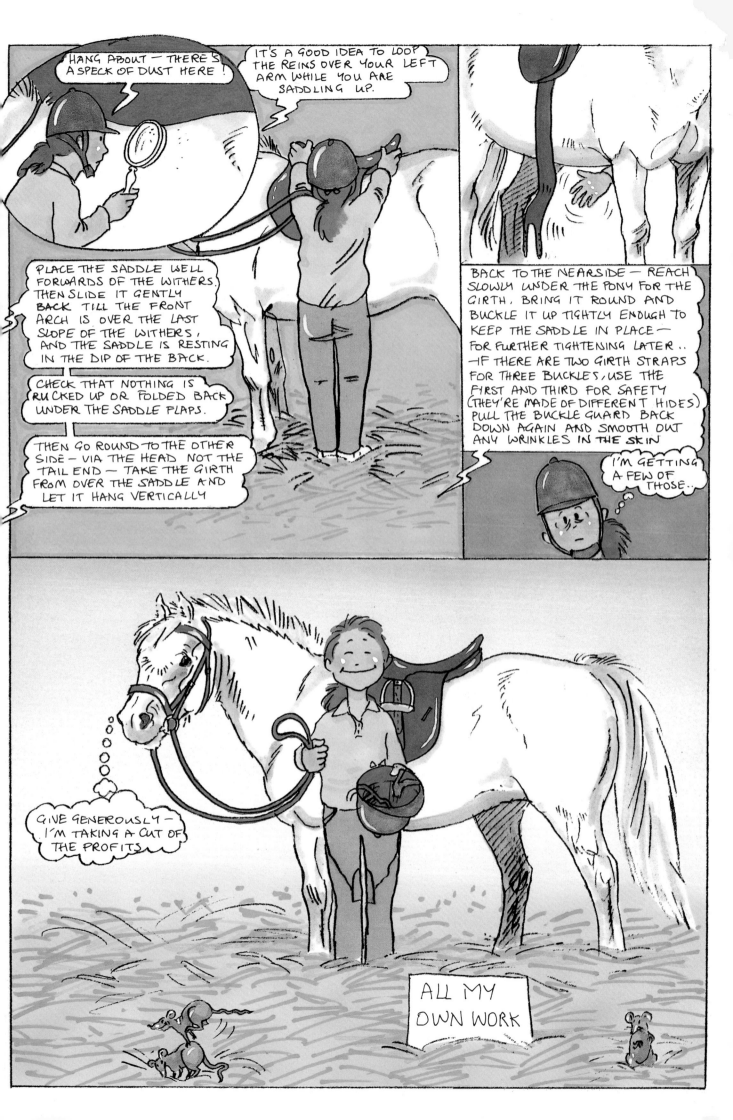

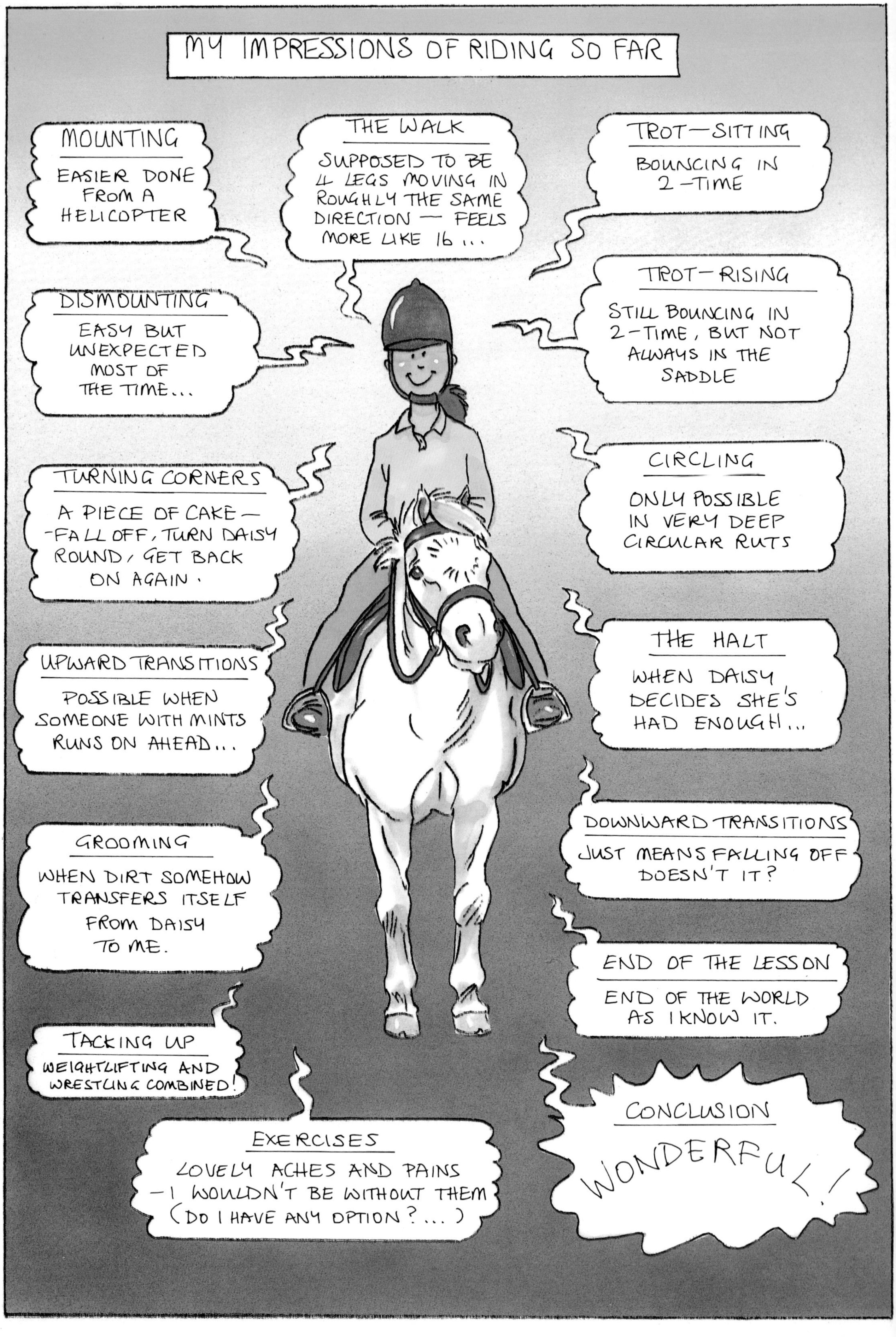
MY IMPRESSIONS OF RIDING SO FAR
MOUNTING
EASIER DONE FROM A HELICOPTER
THE WALK
SUPPOSED TO BE 4 LEGS MOVING IN ROUGHLY THE SAME DIRECTION — FEELS MORE LIKE 16 . . .
TROT—SITTING
BOUNCING IN 2—TIME
DISMOUNTING
EASY BUT UNEXPECTED MOST OF THE TIME . . .
TROT—RISING
STILL BOUNCING IN 2—TIME, BUT NOT ALWAYS IN THE SADDLE
TURNING CORNERS
A PIECE OF CAKE— -FALL OFF, TURN DAISY ROUND, GET BACK ON AGAIN.
CIRCLING
ONLY POSSIBLE IN VERY DEEP CIRCULAR RUTS
UPWARD TRANSITIONS
POSSIBLE WHEN SOMEONE WITH MINTS RUNS ON AHEAD . . .
THE HALT
WHEN DAISY DECIDES SHE'S HAD ENOUGH . . .
GROOMING
WHEN DIRT SOMEHOW TRANSFERS ITSELF FROM DAISY TO ME.
DOWNWARD TRANSITIONS
JUST MEANS FALLING OFF DOESN'T IT?
END OF THE LESSON
END OF THE WORLD AS I KNOW IT.
TACKING UP
WEIGHTLIFTING AND WRESTLING COMBINED!
EXERCISES
LOVELY ACHES AND PAINS -I WOULDN'T BE WITHOUT THEM (DO I HAVE ANY OPTION? . . .)
CONCLUSION
WONDERFUL!

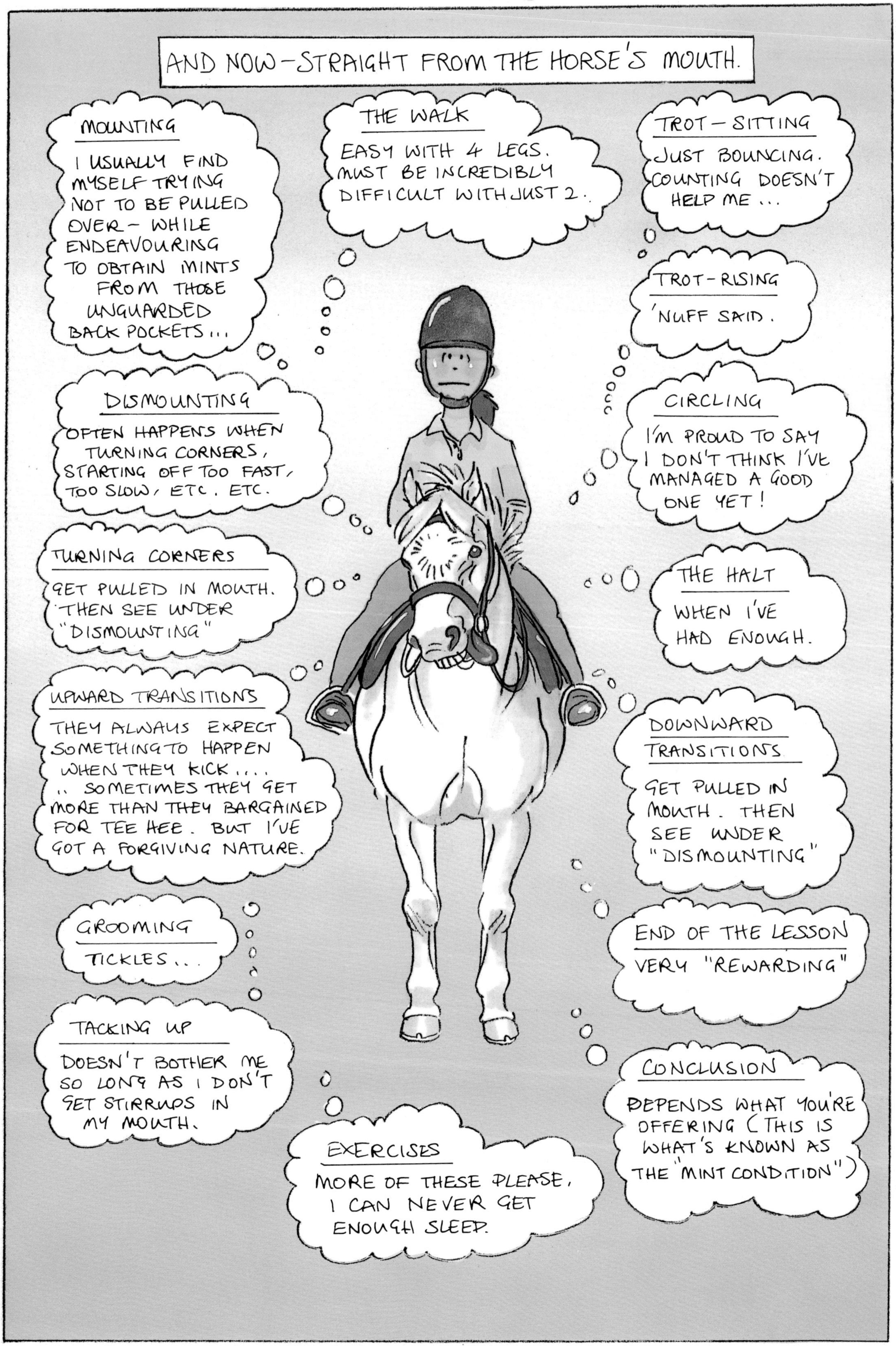
AND NOW – STRAIGHT FROM THE HORSE'S MOUTH.
MOUNTING
I USUALLY FIND MYSELF TRYING NOT TO BE PULLED OVER – WHILE ENDEAVOURING TO OBTAIN MINTS FROM THOSE UNGUARDED BACK POCKETS...
THE WALK
EASY WITH 4 LEGS. MUST BE INCREDIBLY DIFFICULT WITH JUST 2.
TROT – SITTING
JUST BOUNCING. COUNTING DOESN'T HELP ME...
TROT – RISING
'NUFF SAID.
DISMOUNTING
OFTEN HAPPENS WHEN TURNING CORNERS, STARTING OFF TOO FAST, TOO SLOW, ETC. ETC.
CIRCLING
I'M PROUD TO SAY I DON'T THINK I'VE MANAGED A GOOD ONE YET!
TURNING CORNERS
GET PULLED IN MOUTH. THEN SEE UNDER "DISMOUNTING"
THE HALT
WHEN I'VE HAD ENOUGH.
UPWARD TRANSITIONS
THEY ALWAYS EXPECT SOMETHING TO HAPPEN WHEN THEY KICK.... .. SOMETIMES THEY GET MORE THAN THEY BARGAINED FOR TEE HEE. BUT I'VE GOT A FORGIVING NATURE.
DOWNWARD TRANSITIONS
GET PULLED IN MOUTH. THEN SEE UNDER "DISMOUNTING"
GROOMING
TICKLES...
END OF THE LESSON
VERY "REWARDING"
TACKING UP
DOESN'T BOTHER ME SO LONG AS I DON'T GET STIRRUPS IN MY MOUTH.
CONCLUSION
DEPENDS WHAT YOU'RE OFFERING (THIS IS WHAT'S KNOWN AS THE "MINT CONDITION")
EXERCISES
MORE OF THESE PLEASE, I CAN NEVER GET ENOUGH SLEEP.

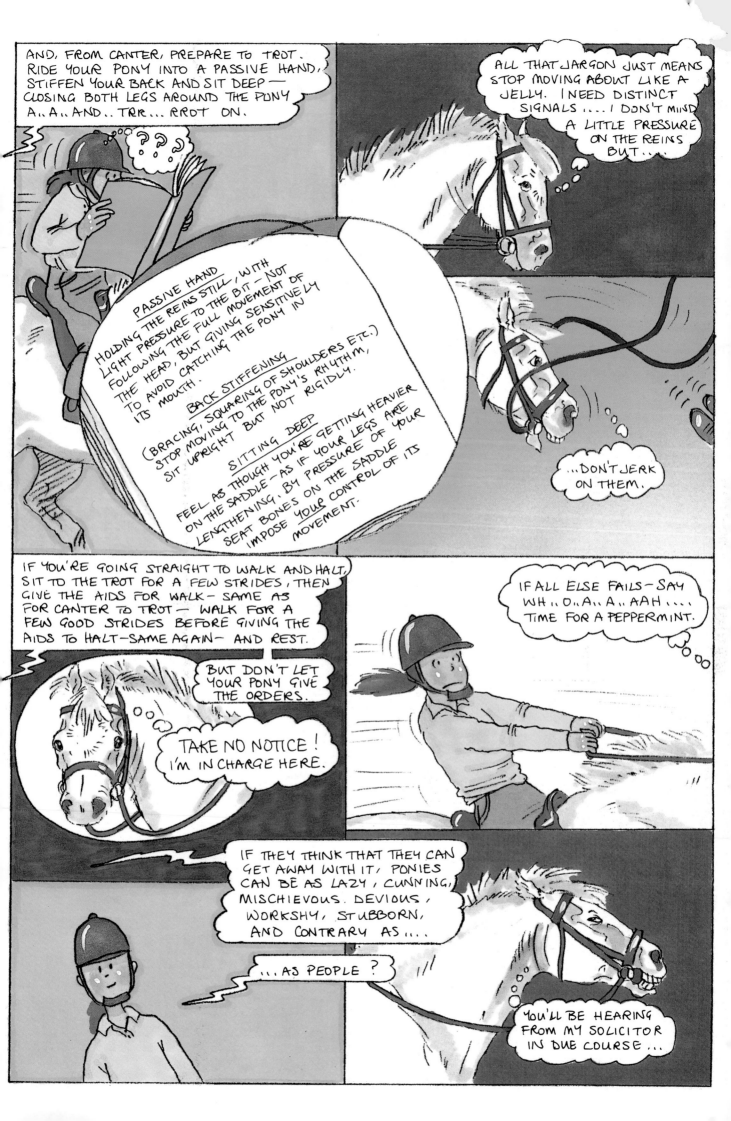

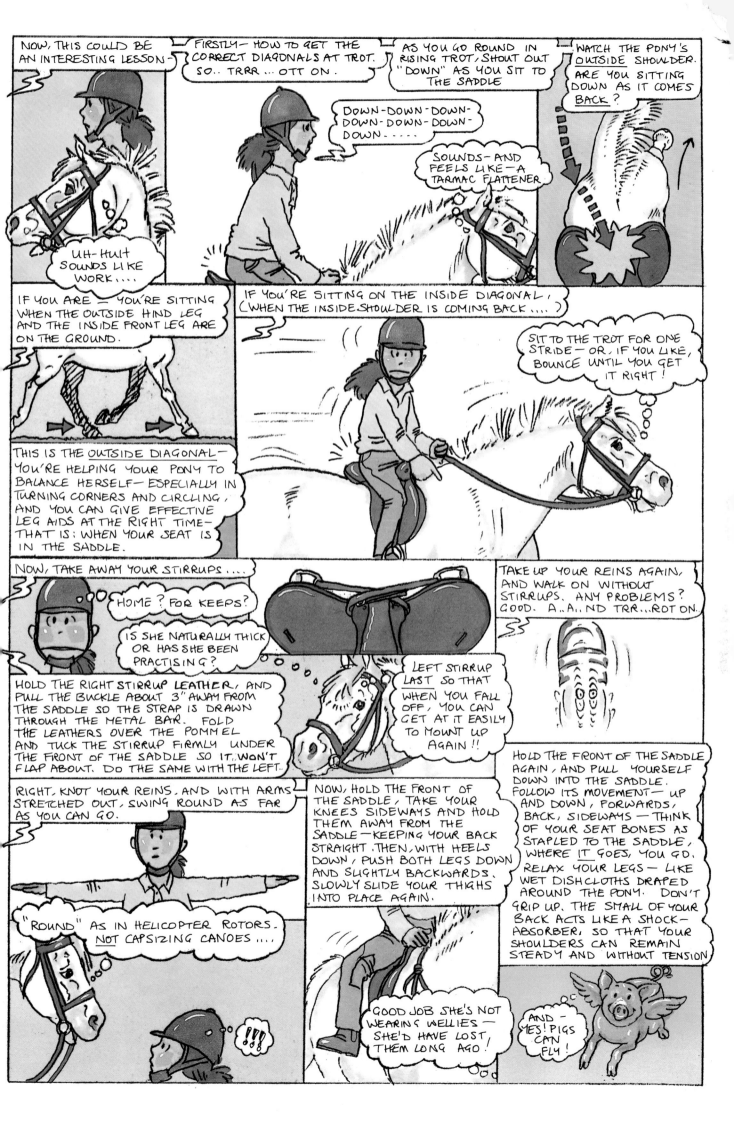

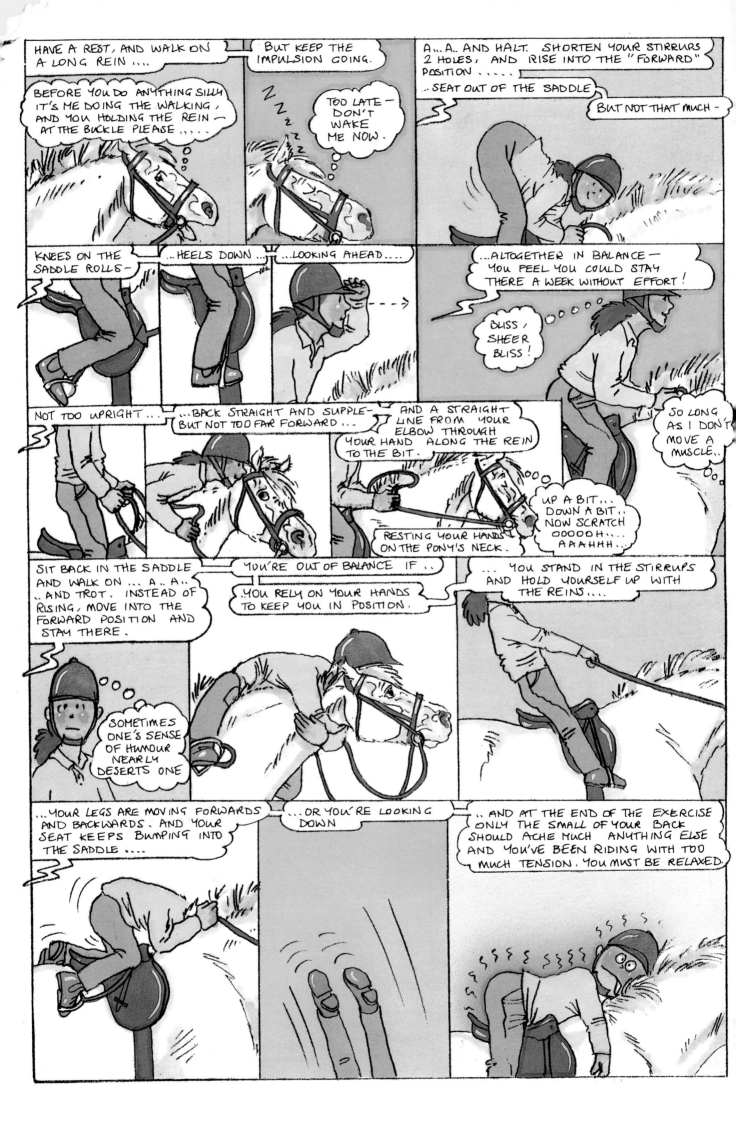

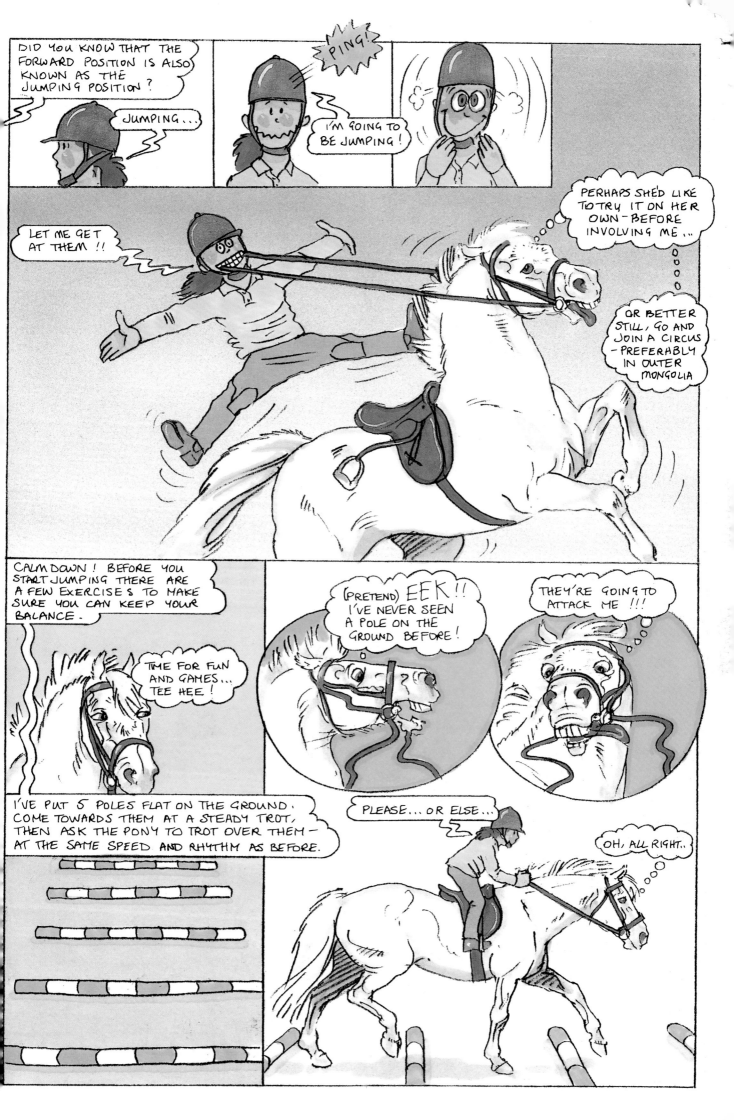

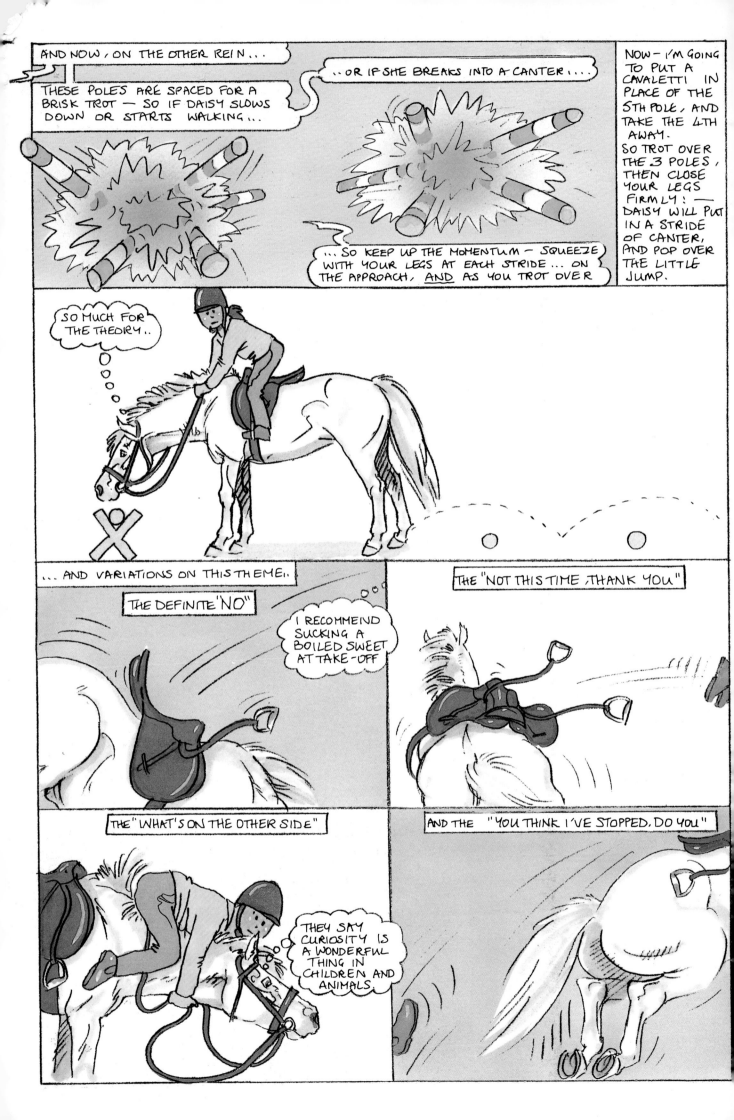

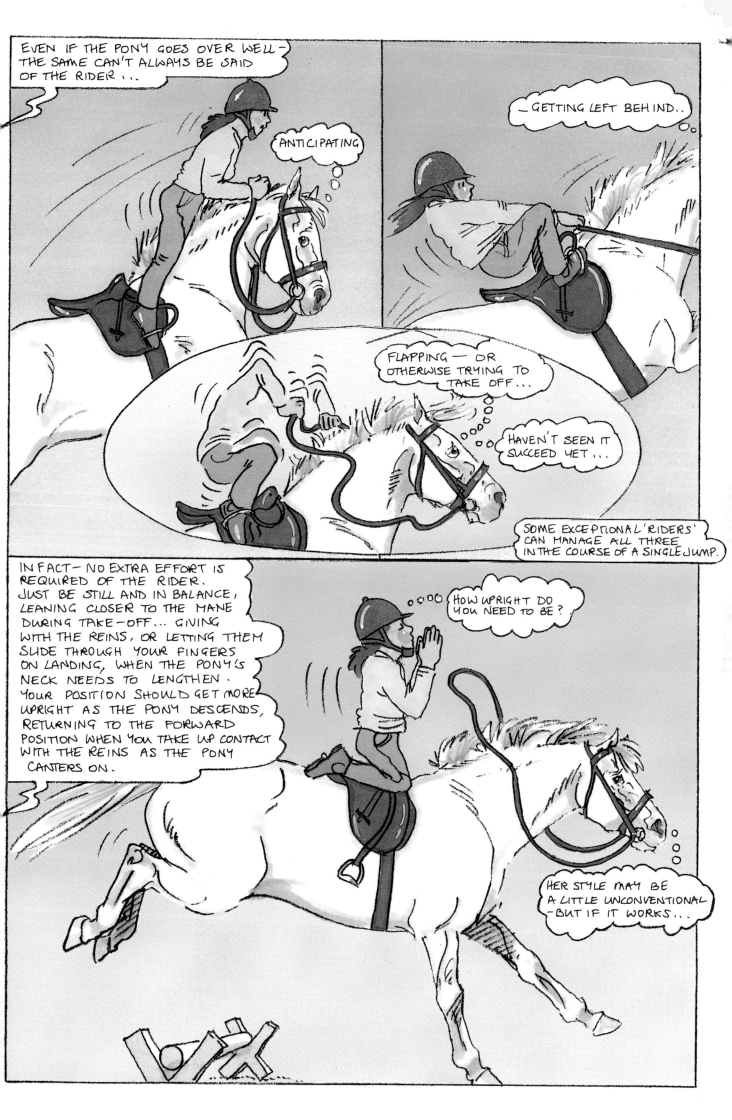

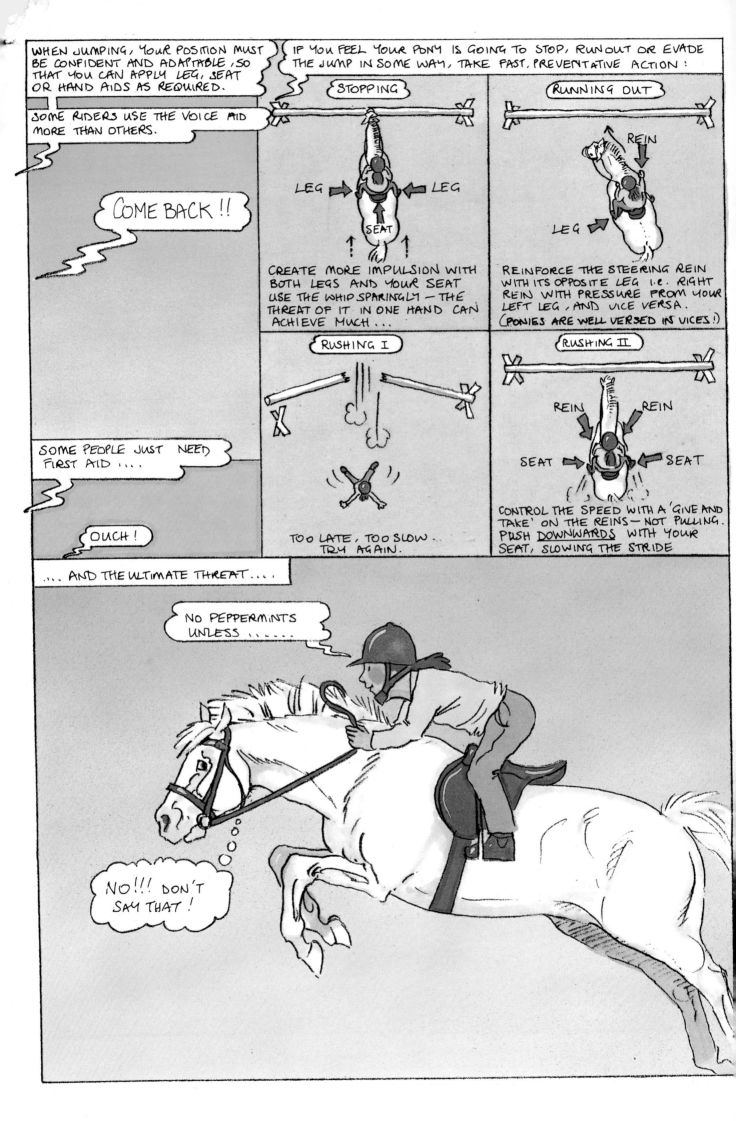

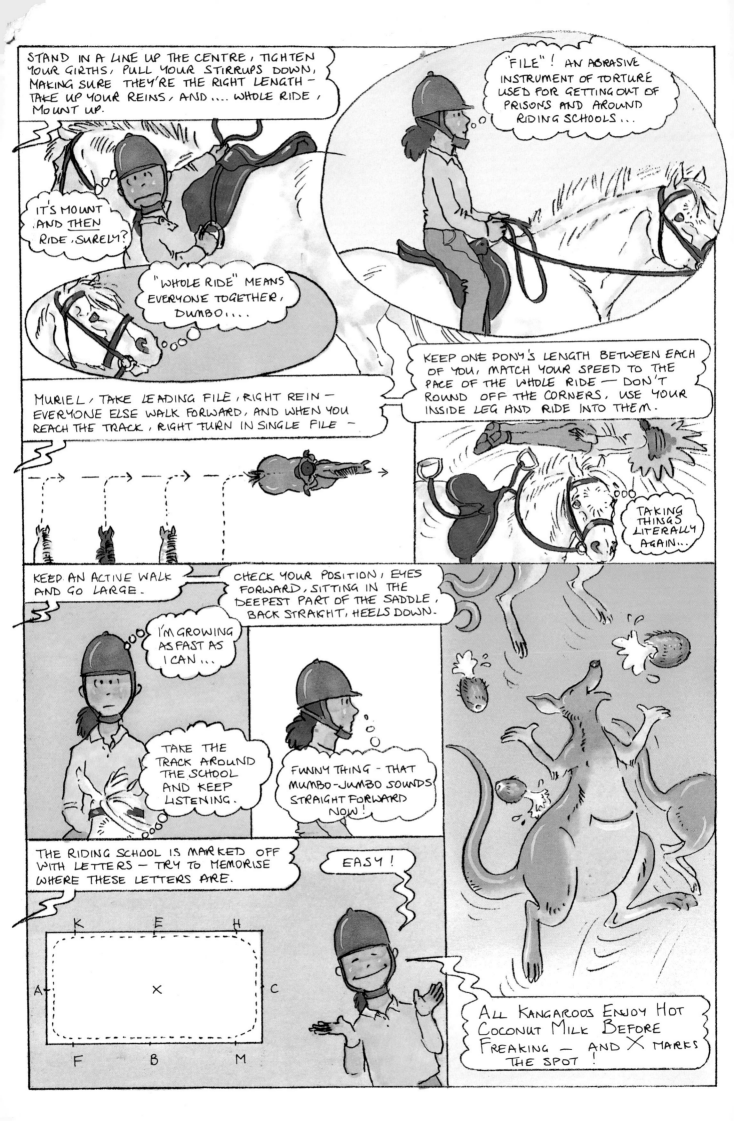

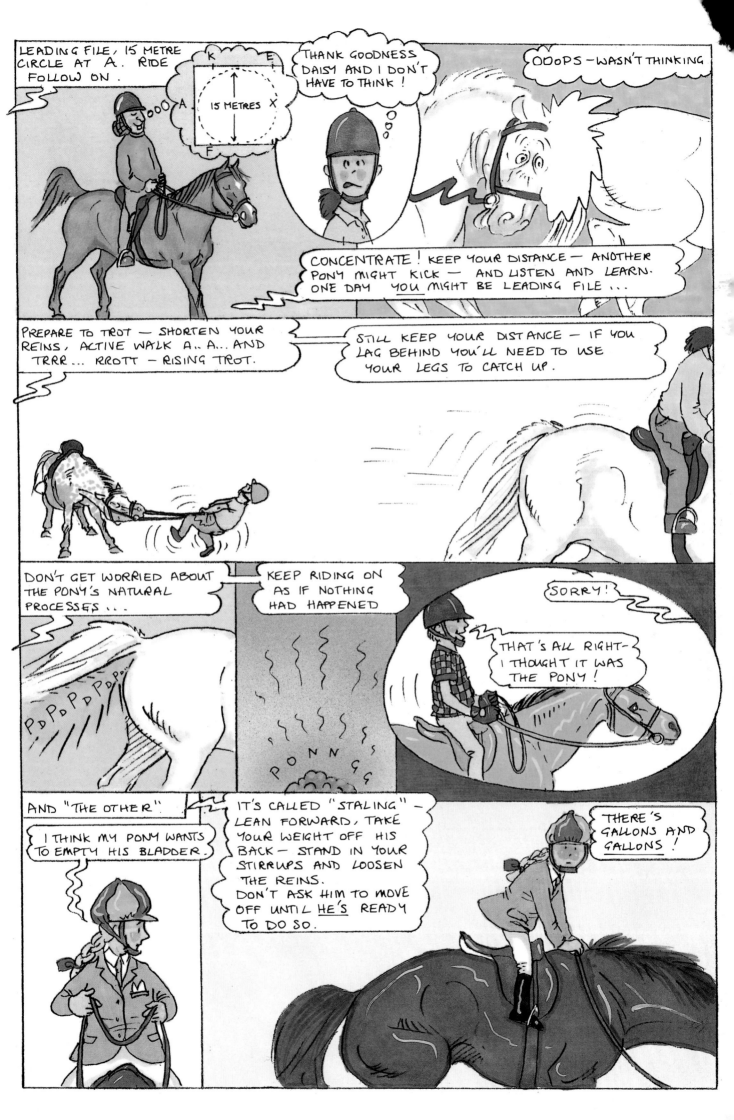

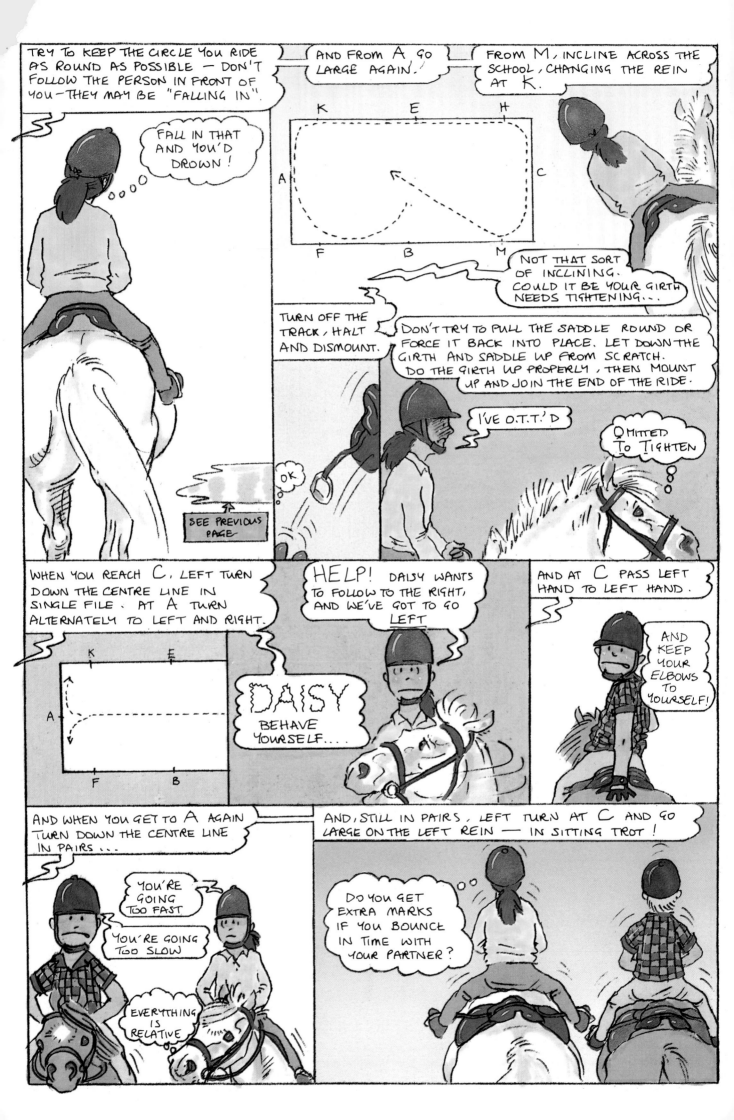

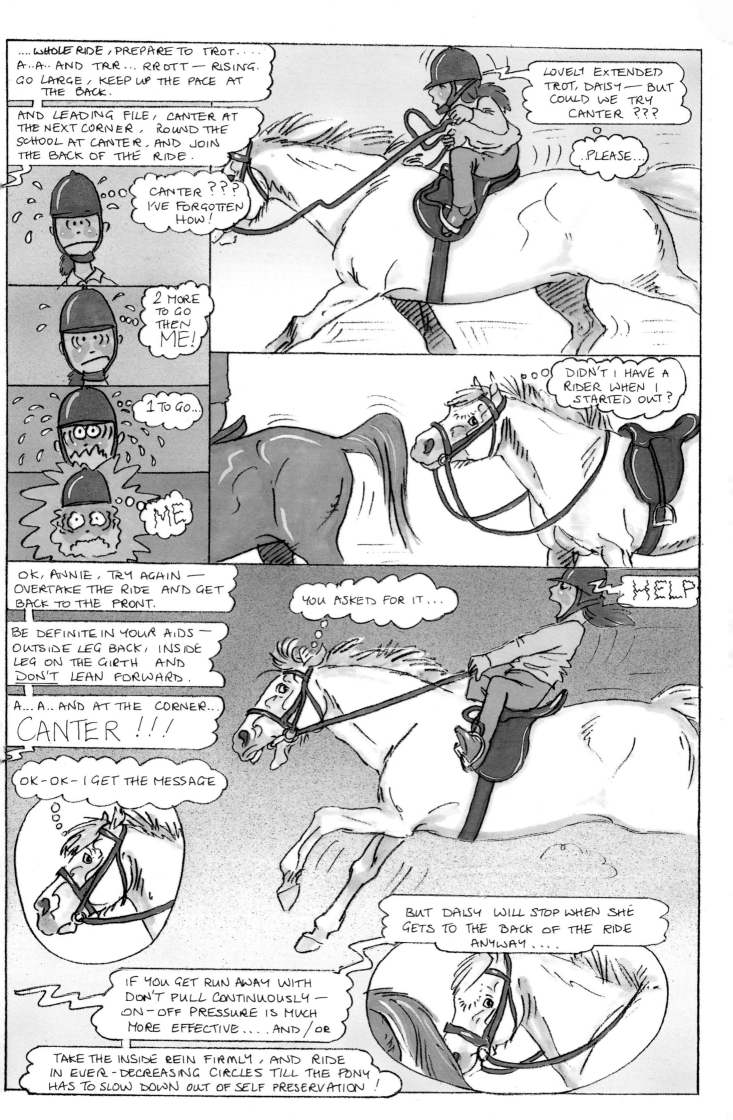

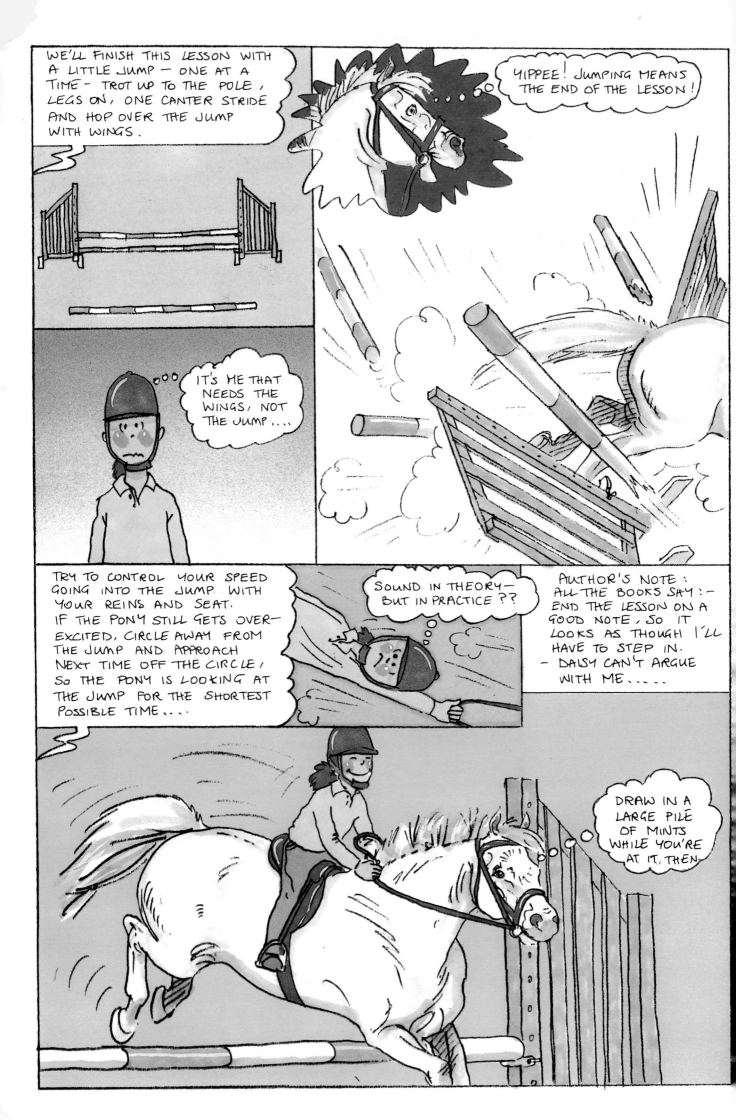